Belmont and the Dragon

The Forest of Doom and Gloom

Mike Zarb
Robin Gold

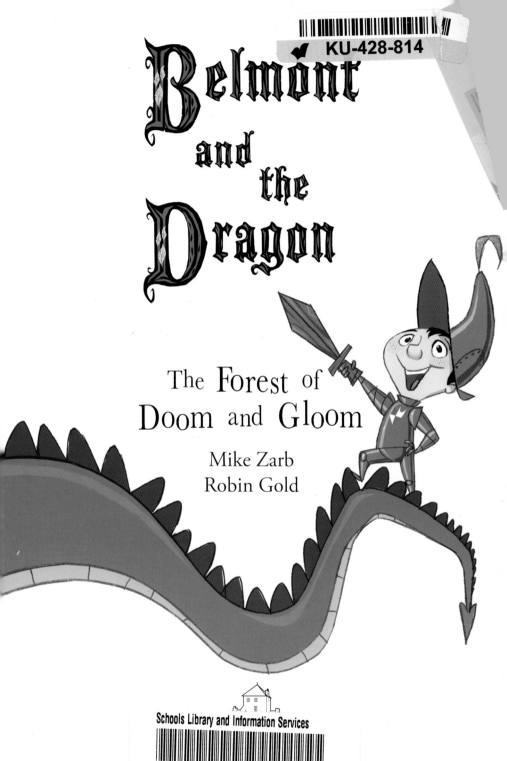

For Mary, and in memory of Paul – MZ

For Judy, Harry and Ben, with love and affection – RG

A Random House book
Published by Random House Australia Pty Ltd
Level 3, 100 Pacific Highway, North Sydney NSW 2060
www.randomhouse.com.au

First published by Random House Australia in 2008
Copyright © Robin Gold 2008
Illustration copyright © Mike Zarb 2008

National Library of Australia
Cataloguing-in-Publication Entry

  Gold, Robin.
    The forest of doom and gloom/Robin Gold ; illustrator,
    Mike Zarb
    ISBN: 9781741663204 (pbk.)
    Series: Belmont and the dragon; 1
    Gold, Robin. Belmont and the dragon; 1.
    For primary school age.
    Other Authors/Contributors: Zarb, Mike.
  A823.4

Cover illustrations by Mike Zarb
Cover and text layout by Jobi Murphy
Printed and bound by Sing Cheong Printing Co. Ltd, Hong Kong
10 9 8 7 6 5 4 3 2 1

Long, long ago, in the mad-cap
medieval metropolis of Old York ...

3

… there lived an orphan boy named Belmont. He was small of stature but in his heart he had a very big dream.

Every day, Belmont stood behind the tall iron gates of the Old York Home for Orphans and Foundlings looking longingly at the castle …

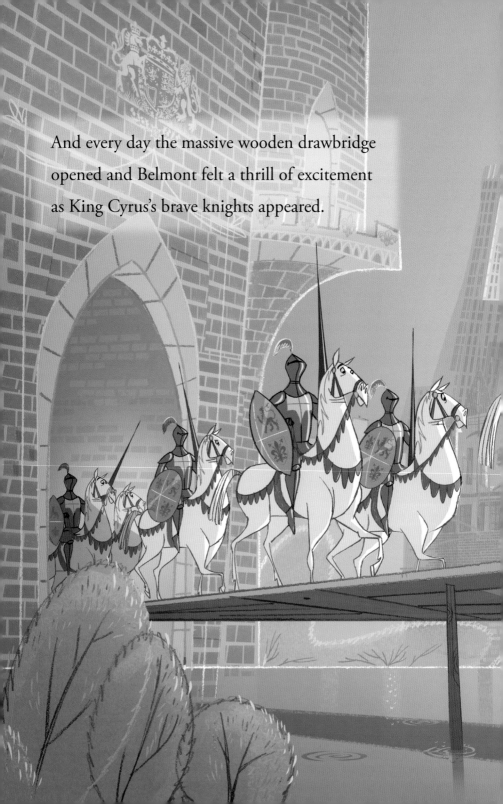

And every day the massive wooden drawbridge
opened and Belmont felt a thrill of excitement
as King Cyrus's brave knights appeared.

Their job was to escort the beautiful Princess Libby on her daily ride in Centaur Park.

The knights looked splendid in their shining armour!
And their magnificent white steeds pranced as
they entered the cobbled streets of
Once Upon a Times Square.

'One day *I'm* going to be a knight!' declared Belmont.

'You? A knight? Don't make me laugh!' snorted a youngster named Spud. 'Knights are big and strong and brave.'

'And they perform heroic deeds like taming dragons and catching witches,' added Zip.

'And they rescue fair damsels in distress,' said Miffy.

'Well then, that's exactly what I
shall do!' said Belmont.

Faster than an Old York minute,
he scooted up a big oak tree and ran
nimbly along a branch.

With a cry of 'GERONIMO!' he leapt into
Once Upon a Times Square and set off on
his quest to become a knight.

To Belmont, Old York was the greatest city in the world. He wouldn't live anywhere else for all the fortune cookies in China!

He loved the bustle of the streets and the ever-changing sights and sounds. The air was filled with the delicious aromas of hotdogs, freshly baked bagels and pizza!

After searching for knightly adventure from Heck's
Kitchen to Madrigal Square Gardens, Belmont found
himself at the edge of Centaur Park, staring at a sign.

14

warning !

You are entering the
Forest of Doom and Gloom
Trespassers will be <u>very</u> sorry
So turn around and GIT!

Ignoring the sign (as any brave knight would) Belmont entered the forest. He was tired and hungry. To his delight, he soon found a prickly bush covered in juicy ripe blackberries.

Meanwhile, in Centaur Park, Princess Libby was bored and managed to escape from her guards. She rode into the forest where they would never think of looking for her …

Belmont was filling his helmet with berries for supper when he heard a twig snap behind the bush. 'A dragon!' he whispered to himself. 'This is my chance.' And with all the strength and courage he could muster, Belmont thrust his toy sword through the thorny branches.

'OW!' yelled Princess Libby, leaping out from behind the bush. 'Who dares prod my royal person?'

'Begging your pardon, princess,' Belmont spluttered. 'I mistook you for a mean ugly dragon.'

'You mistook me for a …WHAT?' demanded the princess, turning an angry shade of crimson.

Belmont was street-wise enough to know that explaining things usually makes matters worse. So he ran away into the forest, not daring to look back.

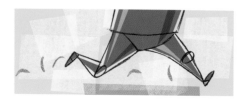

More determined than ever to succeed in his quest,
Belmont marched deeper and deeper into the ghostly,
fog-bound forest.

As he came to a small clearing he heard strange voices arguing. He peeped out from behind a bush and saw a trio of putrid pink pixies laying traps for trespassers. Belmont crept away as quickly and quietly as he could.

'I'll make sure they don't catch me,' he promised himself.

A sudden clap of thunder made him jump, and the first big drops of rain began to fall.

Looking for shelter, Belmont saw the entrance to a dark cave. He crept in as the rain began bucketing down.

Inside, something was snoring loudly. It sounded humungous! Belmont was curious and decided to investigate. As his eyes adjusted to the shadowy gloom of the cave, he suddenly realised it was a …

… fierce, fire-breathing dragon!

As it snored, smoke rings
wafted from its nostrils.

CLANG!
CLANG!

Belmont was so afraid he began to shake. His helmet slipped through his fingers and fell to the ground with a loud clang!

The dragon jumped in fright.

'P-please don't hurt me, mister,' it blubbered.

Belmont was so taken aback that he quite forgot to be frightened.

'How can a great big dragon like you be afraid of a little boy like me? Are you chicken or something?'

'Listen, kid, I ain't no chicken. I'm a S.N.A.D – Sensitive New Age Dragon. And by the way, the name's Burnie.'

'How d'you do. I'm Belmont.'

Just then Burnie noticed the helmet at Belmont's feet.

'What are them black things?' he demanded suspiciously. 'I ain't wearing my contacts! They ain't spiders, are they? I absolutely positively hate sp-sp-spiders,' he added with a shudder.

Belmont laughed. 'They're blackberries. Would you like to share them with me?'

'Thanks, kid,' said Burnie. 'Don't mind if I do.'

From that moment on, Belmont and the dragon got along like a house on fire! They talked and talked until the rain had stopped.

Suddenly, from outside they heard loud screams for help.

Belmont ran to the mouth of the cave and saw the nasty
pink pixies carrying a cage with somebody locked inside.
It was Princess Libby!

'Let me out of here at once, you horrid little beasts!'
she screamed.

'Sorry, sister, no can do,' said Zonk, dragging a comb
through his hair.

'When the Redwitch finds out we've captured the
princess,' grinned Bertha, 'she'll be tickled pink.'

'Yeah … pixie pink!' giggled Chester, his eyes large
behind thick spectacles.

Moments later, a witch in red approached on her flying broomstick. A raven clung tightly to her arm. The broomstick wheezed and spluttered, leaving a trail of filthy black smoke as the Redwitch came in for a perfect two-point landing.

'Well, well, well, what have we here, Silas?' said the Redwitch to the raven. 'If it isn't the royal brat caught like a rat in a trap!'

'You wait 'til Daddy hears about this!' said Princess Libby.

'Seems to me,' said the raven, 'her old man would cough up a tidy little sum just to have her back in one piece.'

'True enough,' said the Redwitch, 'but right now I could use a servant. Someone who can clip my toenails, pluck my nose hairs and clean out my cappuccino machine. I think she'll do very nicely.'

'HELP! Somebody please help!' wailed the princess.

'Unhand that fair damsel at once!' demanded Belmont as he leapt from the cave, brandishing his toy sword.

'Where'd that little squirt come from?' gasped Bertha.

'GERONIMO!' cried Belmont, diving at the pink pixies.

His first blow landed squarely on top of Zonk's head, ruining the pixie's prized hairdo.

'Hey, not the hair. Don't touch the hair!' cried Zonk.

Chester grabbed Belmont from behind. In the scuffle, Chester lost his thick spectacles and fumbled blindly for them on his hands and knees. Bertha thrust her sharp pitchfork at Belmont but he nimbly jumped aside.

'Ouuuuuch!' wailed Chester as the pointy prongs painfully poked his posterior.

Burnie hid in his cave, trembling with fear. Just as
the Redwitch raised her wand to cast an evil spell
on his brave little friend, a tiny spider
dropped onto Burnie's nose.

'EeeeYIIIIIIKES!!!!' roared Burnie, leaping out of the cave with fire shooting from his mouth.

The pixies took one look at Burnie and ran for the hills as fast as their stumpy little legs would carry them.

In the confusion, the Redwitch tripped backwards over a hidden wire. A cage came crashing down, trapping her inside!

'Zonk! Chester! Bertha!' shrieked the Redwitch. 'Come back here, you yellow-bellied pink pipsqueaks!'

But her cowardly minions had vanished over the hill, leaving nothing but a cloud of dust …

That evening, the busy streets and sidewalks of Old York came to a standstill as an unlikely procession marched into Once Upon a Times Square.

Belmont waved to his friends as he passed the Old York Home for Orphans and Foundlings. But all they could do was stare at the boy who had tamed the dragon, captured the witch and rescued the fair damsel!

'For his remarkable acts of bravery,' declared King Cyrus, 'Belmont shall receive a reward of fifty pieces of gold.'

'Sweet shmegeggy! The kid's a zillionaire!' blurted Burnie.

Princess Libby approached the king and whispered something into his ear.

'And at Princess Libby's request,' continued the king, 'I decree that Belmont shall become an honorary knight of the realm.'

The King's brave knights gave a mighty cheer! Belmont couldn't believe his ears. This was a dream come true!

'Atta boy, kid!' cried out Burnie.

And the princess gave Belmont a secret cheeky wink.

Best of all, Belmont and Burnie became great friends. Maybe the best friends ever. And they went on many more adventures together. But that's another story …